FEBOLD FEBOLDSON
THE FIX-IT FARMER

by
Carol Beach York

illustrated by
Irene Trivas

Folk Tales of America

Troll Associates

PROLOGUE

While the United States of America was being settled, people liked to make up stories about how things got to be the way they were. About why the deserts were so hot. Where prairie dogs came from. Things like that, and lots more.

The storytellers had to have a "hero" for their stories. One of their heroes was called Febold Feboldson. They said he was a farmer in Nebraska.

Febold was always trying to be helpful, the storytellers said, and a lot of things might be different today if he hadn't tried to be *quite* so helpful.

Library of Congress # 79-66321
ISBN 0-89375-312-2/0-89375-311-4 (pb)

Febold Feboldson meant well. Everybody always said that. But things didn't always turn out just the way he wanted them to. And that's what caused all the trouble.

Even when Febold was just a chubby farm boy, he had already started trying to be helpful.

Take the time he went on a picnic. Just like today, people loved picnics way back then. The whole Feboldson family went on this one. Grandma, Grandpa, brothers, sisters, everybody. It was a pretty big family, so it was a pretty big picnic. And there was more good food than you could shake a stick at.

The picnic was in a field near a woods, and Febold's mother saw some flowers growing near the trees.

"I sure would like some of those flowers," she said.

Febold thought he could fix that up easy enough. So he trudged off across the field to pick the flowers. He meant well, but he was munching a slice of bread and honey, and he dropped some crumbs as he walked along.

It wasn't two minutes before some wandering ants spotted the crumbs and followed them back across the field.

Pretty soon the ants were right in the middle of the picnic. Right in the middle of all that wonderful food. It was a great day for the ants. They had never found such a feast before.

And you know the rest of *that* story. Ants learned to love picnics. And from that time on, they always come when folks have one. Picnics have never been the same since Febold tried to fix things up.

When Febold was grown, he went to the north woods of Minnesota and landed a job as a cook in Paul Bunyan's lumber camp. Feeding the hungry loggers was a mighty task. The lunch table was so long that the men at one end couldn't see the men at the other end, and it kept 25 cooks busy 25 hours a day feeding them.

Everything was bigger, louder, higher, wider, and faster at Paul Bunyan's camp. The men were stronger and the days were longer.

Most of the food was good, plain food— biscuits and meat and potatoes. There wasn't time to fuss with fancy things. But when Paul Bunyan's birthday came around, Febold fixed a birthday cake.

The cake was so big he had to use hollow logs to pour wax for the candles.

And the cake was so high he had to climb a ladder to light the candles.

Febold meant well—but when he lit up
those giant candles high in the tree tops, he
started the first forest fire. If Paul Bunyan
himself hadn't been there to douse it with
huge buckets of water, the whole state of
Minnesota might not be around today.

While Febold was at Paul Bunyan's camp, the California gold rush of '49 started. Everyone who could hunt up a wagon and horse scrambled out to California as fast as they could go. If they couldn't find a wagon, they'd settle for a horse. They'd settle for a donkey. Anything to get to California.

Some people were lucky in California, and some weren't. But everybody kept right on trying to get there before all the gold was found by someone else.

When Febold Feboldson heard about all this, he turned in his cook's cap, said goodbye to Paul Bunyan, and bought himself a wagon and a team of horses.

But before he could get started, there was a sudden, walloping blizzard on the western plains. Snow came down like an avalanche. Winds roared and howled. Wagons and horses and donkeys were useless in the freezing, swirling snow. It was a sad day for the gold rushers, and they all beat it back to wherever they'd started from, to wait for the blizzard to end.

But after the blizzard quit, there was so much snow on the ground that people still couldn't get across to California.

"We've just got to hang on awhile longer," they said. "That snow has got to melt some- day."

But "someday" never came.

The plains just got colder and colder. And not one flake of snow had melted.

Febold could see that he wasn't going to make much money this way, so he sent to

Death Valley for some good hot sand. Death Valley is about the hottest spot around, and there isn't a better place to get good hot sand, if you happen to need some.

When the sand came, it was almost too hot to handle. But Febold poured it into pails and sold it to the gold rushers.

"Hot sand! Get your hot sand!" Febold shouted as he went through the streets, into the eating places, into the general store. Folks left their card games and their fighting. They woke up from their snoozes by the stove in the corner store.

"I'll take a pail of that!"

"One pail over here!"

"Two pails for me!"

That sand sold faster than cotton candy at a carnival. People were ready to try anything to get to California.

They put the sand on their wagons. People who only had a horse or a donkey tied the sand pails on behind. They drove over the frozen snow with the sand spilling out every which way. The snow began to sizzle and steam. It melted like butter in August.

On to California! the gold rushers shouted.

Everybody patted Febold Feboldson on the back and said how smart he was.

Febold had fixed up the snow all right, but now there was a mess of hot sand lying around on the plains and prairies. That Death Valley sand never did cool off.

And some of the gold rushers never did forgive Febold. Those deserts were hot! Many of them went looking for him on their way back from California. But by that time, Febold was gone. Which was just as well—for even to this day, those hot western deserts are still there. And folks are still complaining.

17

Febold had given up the California idea. He married a woman he met in town when he was selling sand, and he moved to Nebraska with his bride. In Nebraska, Febold bought a farm and a bag of seeds.

Mrs. Feboldson was happy fixing up her new home. Febold was getting all set to plant his first crop, when a bad dry spell came along. A *really bad* dry spell.

There was no rain for days and days.

Weeks and weeks.

Months and months.

The ground was baked too hard and dry to plant even a small seed. Anything that was already planted curled up and died. Cows stood around with their tongues hanging out. Chickens fought for a place in the shade.

There wasn't much for the farmers to do except sit around and hope for rain.

But the dry spell just went on and on.

"Maybe we should give up farming," Mrs. Feboldson said.

But Febold had an idea on how to fix things. "What we need are Indians to dance a rain dance."

Mrs. Feboldson was making pancakes. It was so hot she didn't have to put wood in the stove. She didn't even have to get out her griddle. She just mixed up her batter and poured it on the plates, and the pancakes were ready to eat.

She turned away from her pancakes and looked out at the hot, dry sky. There wasn't a cloud in sight. She'd almost forgotten what a cloud looked like. As far around as she could see, barns, farmhouses, drooping trees, and brown grass were simmering in the sunshine.

"How many Indians do you think it would take?" she asked.

Febold scratched his chin and took a guess. "Oh—maybe ten." But when he looked up at that bare blue sky, he began to think maybe twenty Indians would be more like it. And if twenty was good, thirty might be better. If thirty was better, why not forty . . .?

He finally asked one hundred Indians for help. They gladly came with drums and rattles and rain-dance paint on their faces. Everybody turned out from farm and town to watch as the tribe came in, stirring up clouds of dust on the dry Nebraska roads. It was the most excitement anybody there had seen for a long time. And it was a sight to see.

"Are you sure we needed a *hundred* Indians?" Mrs. Feboldson asked. Everywhere she looked there were Indians.

"You want to stop this dry spell, don't you?" Febold lit up his pipe and settled back to wait for the miracle.

Mrs. Feboldson smoothed her skirts, straightened her sunbonnet, and found herself a good close spot to watch the show. Little children were running around amid the crowd. Mothers were calling to them not to get in the way. Dogs were barking.

"I don't see how those Indians can set their minds to anything with all this racket going on," Mrs. Feboldson said.

But Febold wasn't worried.

"You just watch now," he said. "The rain is coming."

The hundred Indians spread out in a circle. When all was ready, they began to dance and

beat their drums and shake their rattles. And
just like Febold said, the rain came. It poured
down.

And poured down.

And poured down.

"I think maybe a smaller rain dance would
have been enough after all," Mrs. Feboldson
said. "Land a'mercy, we'll all be drowned!"

And still the rain went on, coming down out of the sky like a river. It would have been the Flood and Noah's Ark all over again, if that rain had ever touched the ground. But the air had been so hot and so dry for so long that the heat waves were fifty feet high. As soon as the rain hit those heat waves, it got turned into a thick fog. After that, nobody could see anything.

By the time the rain stopped it was too foggy to plant crops. You couldn't see your own hand in front of your face. People didn't dare go out of their houses for fear of getting lost in the fog. Febold had meant well, but as usual, he'd made things worse than ever.

"Maybe we should give up farming," Mrs. Feboldson said again.

But Febold didn't want to give up.

"You've heard about the fog in London?" he asked his wife.

Mrs. Feboldson supposed she had.

"What do you think they do about it?"

Mrs. Feboldson was sure she didn't know.

"Why, they cut it up," Febold said. "What we need is something to cut up this fog."

And without more ado, he sent away to London for a fog-cutter. This was a clanky contraption that looked like a giant pair of scissors on wheels. Mrs. Feboldson still said they should move out of Nebraska—if they could see which way was *out*. But Febold hitched up his horse lickety-split and drove all around cutting up the fog into long thin slices.

People began to come out of their houses again. They began to plow their fields. Everybody was happy—except Febold. He wanted to start planting his crops too, but he had all those strips of fog to get rid of.

"What am I going to do with all this fog?" He was sputtering around, fit to be tied.

"You can't dump it in the fields," Mrs. Feboldson said. "Folks are plowing and planting there."

"I can see that," Febold said. "I should be plowing and planting, too."

But there was still that fog. Long, skinny, slippery slices of it, stacked up like firewood in Febold's barnyard.

"I sure wish you'd take it somewhere else," Mrs. Feboldson said. She tried to be patient, but those piles of fog were hard to put up with.

"Somewhere else is the best place for it," Febold agreed. He piled the strips of fog on his wagon, hitched up his horse, and made a lot of trips up and down Nebraska, laying out the pieces of fog at the sides of the roads.

That worked pretty well. The fog slowly settled down into the ground and disappeared. Once again Febold had fixed things.

But every spring when the ground warms up, the fog gets wet and messy. Nebraska roads can be very muddy, and people have to kind of wade along when they want to go someplace.

What was worse, with the fog out of the way, the grasshoppers could see what fine crops the Nebraska farmers were raising. They began to come more fast and furious than—well, than

ants at a picnic. The grasshoppers ate everything that was growing, and some things that weren't.

They ate Febold's best shirt off the laundry line, and then they ate the line. Mrs. Feboldson had no place to hang her wash. She had grasshoppers jumping out of her cupboards and sitting in her hats.

She was ready to move again.

But Febold sent for some flying fish. And they ate the grasshoppers; a tasty meal.

The flying fish were a nuisance afterward, so Febold had to send for timber wolves to eat the flying fish.

After that he sent away for cottonwood trees, so the timber wolves would feel at home.

"Seems to me one thing just leads to another," Mrs. Feboldson said.

When the cottonwood trees bloomed, fluffy

scraps of white cotton were floating in the air everywhere. Nebraska didn't look very tidy, so Febold fixed that up by sending away for people to pick the cotton.

They picked the cotton on the lower branches, but the top branches were too high to reach.

"We can fix that," Febold said. "If the pickers can't get to the tree tops, we'll bring the tree tops to the pickers."

Meaning well again, he sent away for strong ropes and stakes. He tied the tops of the trees down onto the ground, and the people were able to pick the cotton all right—but the cottonwood trees began to grow down into the ground.

And the timber wolves burrowed down after the trees.

The wolves didn't get any sunshine or fresh air underground, and they began to get small and puny.

"Those wolves are shrinking away to nothing," Mrs. Feboldson said. "They're no bigger than little dogs now."

And she was right.

People took up her words and began calling the timber wolves "prairie dogs." Their holes were all over and their underground tunnels crisscrossed miles and miles of land. "We can hardly find a good solid place to plant crops," the farmers grumbled. Things looked bad again.

"What we need are some mirrors to reflect sunshine down into those burrows," Febold said. He never ran out of ideas. "And we need some wind machines to blow fresh air down there. When those prairie dogs grow back to their natural size, they'll come up out of the holes."

We'll never know how that plan would have worked, for just about that time ("in the nick of time" some people might say), Febold got a letter from California.

It seems that after the big gold rush calmed down, folks in California had time to listen to other news. They had heard about Febold Feboldson, the fix-it-up farmer.

They had heard that Febold helped Nebraska through a dry spell. They had heard he cleared up a fog. They had heard he rid the farmers of grasshoppers and beautified the countryside with trees. It all sounded wonderful. (Some details had been left out, though. The folks in California hadn't heard about the muddy roads and the prairie dogs.) They thought Febold was just the man they needed. The letter said,

There has been too much going wrong out here in California. A big earthquake for one. And people tearing up the land looking for gold. We want you to come and fix it up.

Mrs. Feboldson had never forgotten the grasshoppers in her hats. She was still struggling with muddy roads and fields filled with prairie-dog holes. When she read the letter from California, she thought they'd sent for the wrong man.

But she also thought any place would be better than a farm cluttered up with the mirrors and wind machines Febold was going to send for. So she kept her mouth shut.

Febold strutted around a bit after that letter. It was enough to make a man right proud.

He packed up his belongings, sold his farm, and set out for California, with Mrs. Feboldson riding along on the wagon seat with the fog-cutter tied on behind. Just in case there was fog in California. Off they went over the muddy roads and prairie-dog holes. No one in Nebraska ever saw them again.

Of course, you know the first thing Febold did in California. He began sending away for

things. He was always great for that. He sent away for some palm trees from the South Seas and some warm air from South America. And that was just for a start.

We don't know all the things he sent away for to fix up California, but his ideas worked out fairly well. Even Mrs. Feboldson had to admit it was so. California kept on getting better and better.

Of course, it isn't perfect even now, but it's pretty good. Better than a lot of places you can think of. People began flocking to California to live, and they're still flocking.

But ants are still coming to picnics.

All that Death Valley sand is still sizzling on the western plains.

And the folks in Nebraska never did get rid of the prairie dogs.